Core Knowledge Language Arts®

Sir Gus

Unit 5 Reader

Skills Strand

GRADE 2

Amplify learning.

Core Knowledge®

ISBN 978-1-61700-211-3

© 2013 Core Knowledge Foundation
www.coreknowledge.org

Printed in the USA
NA05 LSCOW 2017

Table of Contents
Sir Gus
Unit 5 Reader

Sir Gus and His Stuff

This reader tells the tale of Sir Gus, a knight. In the past, there really were knights like Sir Gus. Knights helped kings and queens keep their lands safe. Here are some of the things a knight would have used.

Lance

Sir Gus

Shield

Spear

Sword

Knights rode on horses and helped defend castles.

Sir Gus

Knight

Castle

The Beginning

Long before you were born, in a place we can no longer find, there was a king. King Alfred was his name.

King Alfred was in charge of a large land that stretched from the dark forests of the north to the sea in the south. The people of this land were very happy with him as their king. King Alfred liked to have fun. He liked parties and feasts. He was fair and kind, and he kept his people safe.

King Alfred could not do this all by himself. He had twelve knights to help him keep his lands peaceful and his people safe. These brave knights—well, sometimes they were brave—helped to keep bad things from happening.

The most well-known knight of all was Sir Gus the Fearless. The king himself had given Sir Gus the name "Fearless." This was an odd name, for Sir Gus was not entirely fearless. In fact, he had a lot of fears.

Sir Gus was scared of the dark. He was scared of mice and bats and spiders. He did not like boats and he could not swim. Shadows and loud noises made him faint. In fact, lots of things made Sir Gus faint.

Sir Gus had all the things a knight must have. He had a shield and a lance. He had a spear and a sword. But Sir Gus liked a long soak in a bathtub better than a fight.

Cats and horses made Sir Gus itch. Sometimes the itching was so bad that he would start jumping up and down.

Sir Gus was rather absentminded. He got lost a lot and could rarely tell which way to go. Sir Gus found it difficult to get up in the morning. He liked to sleep in, so he was late most of the time.

All in all, Sir Gus was a rather odd knight. But King Alfred did not see this. What he saw was that Sir Gus always served him well.

The Thief

One dark and stormy night while King Alfred was sleeping, a thief crept into his bedroom and stole the king's golden ring. The next morning, when the king woke up, he saw that his ring was gone!

The king was very sad.

"Someone stole my ring!" he cried in agony. "It was my father's ring, and his father's before him. It is a king's ring. I must have it back!"

King Alfred was so upset in the morning; he could not eat his herring on toast.

King Alfred summoned his twelve brave knights. Eleven of them came at once on horseback. Sir Gus the Fearless came later, on foot. Sir Gus explained why he was late. He explained that he had lost his horse.

"Why, good sir," said the king, "you will not get very far on foot!"

"Yes, my lord. I mean no, my lord," replied Sir Gus. "The problem is, your majesty, that when I am on my horse, I itch. I had such a bad itch last night that I fell off my horse and it ran off."

"Well, you must stop itching then," said the king.

"Yes, indeed," replied Sir Gus, trying very hard not to itch.

Then the king told the knights what had happened. He told them he was counting on them to recover his ring.

The next day, at sunrise, eleven of the knights galloped off to find the thief.

Some time after lunch, Sir Gus was awakened by the king himself.

"Not up yet?" asked the king.

"Pardon me, my lord," stammered Sir Gus. "I was just…"

"Nevermind!" said the king. "There's no need to explain. Why should you be up at the crack of dawn? For what can a knight do without a horse? But never fear! I have a gift for you. You may take my horse. But you must be careful, Sir Gus. My horse is the fastest in the land."

Sir Gus got out of bed. He stretched and yawned loudly. Then he got dressed.

"Do not fear," said Sir Gus, as he mounted the horse. "I am an—"

And with that, Sir Gus was carried off. The king's horse had shot off like an arrow.

Sir Gus went to draw water from the well. He grabbed the rope and began to tug on it. But then he felt the need to scratch. He let go of the rope and started itching himself. Soon he was scratching himself so hard that he started jumping up and down. He jumped up and down so much that he fell into the well and landed with a splash at the bottom.

"Ack!" cried Sir Gus. "What have I done?"

It was a good thing that Sir Gus was tall. The water in the well only came up to his chest.

The young man peered down into the well.

"Have no fear!" he shouted to Sir Gus. "I will help you. I will drop the bucket down. Take hold of it, and I will lift you up."

Sir Gus waited nervously at the bottom of the dark well. He did not like the dark or the cold water. His legs began to shiver and shake.

The bucket came down the well. Sir Gus grabbed the bucket and held on tight.

Slowly the young man began to bring Sir Gus up out of the well.

As Sir Gus reached the top of the well, the young man offered the knight his hand.

"Young man," said Sir Gus, as he stepped out of the well, "I am touched by your generous deed. I would like to thank you for helping me. What is your name?"

"My name is Robin," replied the man.

"Well, then, Robin," said Sir Gus, "I thank you."

"You are welcome," said Robin.

The two men shook hands. Robin clasped the knight's hand so tightly that water dripped from his glove.

Robin smiled. "Come into my house," he said. "I will find you some dry clothing."

Sir Gus went inside.

"Sit down," said Robin. "I will fetch you some dry clothing and something to drink." Robin left the room.

Sir Gus sat down on a wooden chair. As he did so, a large black cat jumped onto his lap. At once, Sir Gus began to itch all over. He got up and started jumping up and down. He jumped so hard that he knocked over a chair and bumped into a shelf.

Some things fell off the shelf. As he bent down to pick these things up, Sir Gus spotted a ring. It was the king's ring! Robin was the robber!

Sir Gus stood thinking for a moment.

"There is no point fighting with the man," Sir Gus said to himself. "That would be dangerous. I can tell by his grip that he is very strong."

Sir Gus grabbed the ring. Then he tiptoed quietly out of the house. He mounted his horse and rode back to see the king.

The Hungry Troll

King Alfred was delighted when Sir Gus gave him his ring.

"How did you find it so quickly?" he asked.

Sir Gus shrugged and said, "It was nothing, sire—just a bit of good luck."

"I see you are not only brave and clever," said the king. "You are modest as well!"

The king slipped the ring back on his finger. Then he had all his other knights come to a meeting.

"Knights," he said, "brave Sir Gus has recovered my ring. You may all go home."

The knights rode off to their homes in the country. They carried with them the story of Sir Gus and the king's ring. The story was told far and wide. Sir Gus became a very famous knight.

For a long time, all was well. Each day the king would hunt, fish, and eat. Each night he slept peacefully in his bed.

Months passed. Then one snowy winter morning, there came the sound of thunder. Except it was not thunder. It was the thunderous cry of a troll.

The troll had woken from a long sleep. It was very hungry. A troll is a monstrous beast. It will eat a lot of things, but it is very fond of people.

King Alfred was frightened. He woke up when the troll cried out. He feared for the safety of his kingdom. He sent for his knights.

At once, eleven brave knights came. They too were woken by the loud cry of the troll.

However, Sir Gus the Fearless did not come. The cries of the troll had not woken him. He was still tucked up in bed snoring. At last, the king could wait no longer. He sent one of the other knights to fetch Sir Gus.

Sometime after lunch, Sir Gus came. He was tired and hungry. He had a bad cold. His nose was swollen and red.

"What kept you?" asked the king. "Did you not hear the sound of the troll?"

"*Doe*, your *dajesty*," said Sir Gus, "I did *dot*. I have a *dold* in my *doze*," replied Sir Gus.

"Well it must have stopped up your ears, too!" said the king. "Hear me, knights! I am concerned. We must do something to stop this monstrous troll! We must keep this loathsome beast from eating all of the people in my kingdom! Who has a plan?"

"If I may, your majesty," said the knight known as Sir Tom, "I know that trolls are scared of fire. We could make a fire near the troll's home and scare it."

"I like it!" said the king. "See that it is done!"

Eleven of the knights went to get torches. Then they rode off to find the troll.

Sir Gus, however, did not ride off at once. He crept into the king's kitchen and helped himself to a big slice of pie.

Fire!

It was not hard to find the troll. Trolls cry when they are hungry. The knights simply followed the sound of loud sobs and eating.

As nightfall neared, the knights arrived at the foot of a large hill. The troll had spent all day eating the rocks and plants on the hill. All that was left on the hill were some prickly plants and some old, dying trees.

Near the top of the hill was a cave. Scary troll sounds were coming from inside the cave.

The knights met in a grove at the foot of the hill. They knelt down and made a plan.

"When it is dark we will light our torches," said Sir Tom. "Then we will creep up the hill. The sight of the flames will scare the troll and it will go back to its home beneath the ground."

"And what if that plan fails?" asked Sir Ed. "I don't care to be the troll's dinner."

"Well, do you have a better plan?" asked Sir Tom.

Sir Ed said nothing. The other knights were quiet, as well.

At that very moment came the sound of a horse trotting nearby.

"Found you at last!" said Sir Gus as he rode up to the knights. "So, my fellow knights, tell me, have you devised a plan of attack to defeat this monstrous troll?"

"Yes, we have!" said Sir Tom. "We have agreed that our bravest knight will creep up the hill with a torch and frighten the troll away."

"Splendid idea!" said Sir Gus. "And who is going to attempt this brave deed?" he asked, looking around.

"You!" said Sir Tom and Sir Ed together.

"But, but... well... I... er... um...," said a reluctant Sir Gus.

It was no good trying to get out of it. Sir Tom handed Sir Gus a lit torch. Then he pointed at the cave.

49

Sir Gus went up the hill alone. By the time he reached the mouth of the cave, it was pitch black. The lit torch cast shadows on the ground.

Sir Gus looked around him. He saw shadows dancing on the ground. He was afraid. But he pressed on.

From inside the cave came alarming troll sounds.

"Snnniccck, Snnnuummm, Guffumffffff!"

The troll was eating bits of rock with its sharp teeth, then spitting out the bits it did not like.

Sir Gus approached the cave. Small pieces of rock came flying out. Some of them landed at Sir Gus's feet. Sir Gus jumped back, trying to avoid the flying pieces of rock.

Sir Gus lay on the ground for a while. At last the heat from the fire woke him. He got up and ran back down the hill.

When Sir Gus appeared, the knights shouted, "Hooray! Brave Sir Gus lit the fire! He has driven away the troll! Hooray for Sir Gus!"

The Boat Trip

Word of how Brave Sir Gus had driven away the troll went across the kingdom. The tale soon reached King Alfred. The king was so grateful to Sir Gus that he changed his name from Sir Gus the Fearless to Sir Gus the Utterly Fearless. Sir Gus was given a splendid, but rather large, red robe to keep as a symbol of his bravery.

To celebrate the defeat of the troll, the king invited his knights to go hunting with him. Eleven of the knights rode off with the king to hunt for red deer and wild pigs. Sir Gus, however, didn't go. He did not like hunting. It was far too dangerous.

Rather than go hunting, Sir Gus took a long, relaxing bath. Then he went to the kitchen to see what tasty foods were being prepared.

The next day, King Alfred decided to go sailing on his boat. He insisted that his knights all go with him. And so, right after lunch, the knights made their way south to the coast. One by one they stepped onto the king's boat.

Sir Gus wanted to tell the king that he did not like boats or water. In fact, the two together made him very sick indeed. But he didn't want to upset the king, so he joined the party.

It was a nice afternoon when the boat set sail. The sun shone. The water was calm. There was not a cloud in the sky.

The king appeared on deck.

"Isn't this wonderful?" he said. "Sir Gus, I trust you are having a wonderful time?"

"Yes, indeed, I am," replied Sir Gus, lying.

Then, late in the afternoon, the sky darkened. The wind began to blow. Large waves began to beat on the side of the boat. Sir Gus began to feel ill.

The king was alarmed. He and eleven of the knights had to fight to keep the boat afloat in the strong winds and rising waves.

As for Sir Gus, he was so sick he no longer cared if the boat floated or sank. He couldn't stand up. He lay in the bottom of the boat moaning and groaning.

And that is why no one saw the large pirate ship approaching.

The King's Ghost

"Ar! Do as we say or die!" came the sound of a large booming voice from somewhere on the water.

King Alfred and eleven of his knights jumped with fright. They had all tried to sail the boat in the stormy waves and strong winds. They looked up to see a pirate ship flying a black flag. The pirate ship had sailed up next to the king's boat.

The king and the eleven knights were not prepared to fight. The knights did not have their swords or shields with them.

"I will count to ten," shouted the pirate chief. "If you do not hand over the king and his boat by then, we will attack! We do not care to harm you, but if we must, then we must!"

The pirate chief began to count, "One, two... um." He hesitated. (Pirates aren't good at math!)

"Three," came a voice from below. It was Sir Gus. He was lying down below the deck, and he was feeling very ill.

Sir Gus was so ill that he had no idea what was happening. The strong winds had kept him from hearing what the pirate chief had said. All he could make out was the sound of someone counting.

"Thank you," said the pirate chief. He went on counting. "Seven, eight, nine..."

"Uuuuuug! Ooooooe!" came a loud and scary sound from inside King Alfred's boat.

Not long after, the clouds cleared and the waves died down. Sir Gus felt some relief and came limping back up on deck.

"Well done, Sir Gus!" said the king. "You scared those evil pirates away by pretending to be a ghost."

"I did?" said Sir Gus, still looking rather green in the face.

"Why, yes!" said the king. "Such a clever and helpful trick! How can I ever repay you for your wisdom and bravery? Perhaps I should award you a medal?"

"Your majesty," said Sir Gus, "the best payment of all would be if you would order the captain to sail this boat back to land. I find the nautical life not to agree with me."

And with that, the king's boat sailed for home.

69

The Letter

The story of how Sir Gus saved the king from pirates traveled across the land. People began to tell tales of Brave Sir Gus.

The king thanked his knights and gave them presents. Sir Gus was given a shiny medal and a silver cup. Then, after several parties at the palace, the knights went back to their homes.

The kingdom remained peaceful and calm for several months. Then one day, the king was given a letter that told of danger.

The King summoned his knights to the palace. Just as before, eleven of the twelve knights arrived at once. However, it was several days before Sir Gus the Utterly Fearless appeared, looking dazed and dented.

"I am glad to see that you have arrived at last," said the king.

Sir Gus knelt down.

"Your majesty, I apologize for my late arrival. I had a nasty run-in with a llama near the Old Stone Bridge," explained the knight.

"A llama?" exclaimed the king. "I didn't know that we had llamas in our kingdom."

"Indeed, nor did I, your majesty," replied Sir Gus.

Then the king called an assembly of all of his brave knights.

"Good knights," said the king, "my people have told me that there is a fearsome beast in the Bleak Forest of the East. It is said that this beast can make flames come out of its mouth. Which of you noble knights will do battle with this terrible beast?"

Sir Gus was looking at a fly buzz around the room, so he did not hear much of what the king said. He did not see that his fellow knights had all taken a step back, leaving him standing alone in front of the king.

"Once again, Sir Gus the Utterly Fearless will save us!" proclaimed the king, as he patted the rather astonished knight on the back.

Sir Gus looked puzzled.

The other knights smiled and chuckled.

The Fearsome Beast

The next morning, long after everyone else had eaten their morning meal, Sir Gus awoke, much rested but not eager to set off. He yawned. He stretched. He took a bath. He had lunch. At last, he mounted his horse. But he soon faced another problem: he could not tell which way was east.

Sir Gus could seldom tell which way to travel. He rarely saw the morning sun, so he did not know that it rose in the east. But knowing that he did indeed need to begin, he sniffed the afternoon air, flipped a coin, and rode north.

Sir Gus rode north into the Woods of Doom. He rode for a week. The days got shorter and colder. Sir Gus did not know why.

Another thing Sir Gus did not know was that the Woods of Doom were very dangerous. So he was not prepared when, from out of nowhere, there appeared a band of armed men. The men were bandits. They grabbed Sir Gus and tied him up.

The bandits bundled Sir Gus into the back of a wagon. Then, with much speed, they began to travel southeast.

About a week later, the bandits arrived at the Bleak Forest of the East. There, not far from the Dark Dismal Swamp, they made camp. The bandits had some dinner and went to sleep.

The next morning, while the bandits were still sleeping, something deep inside the forest began to creep closer to their camp. It was the fearsome beast. It had eyes of red flame. It had claws that could shred the hardest stone. It shot fiery flames that could melt metal. And it was going to pounce on the sleeping men.

Sir Gus had relaxed for the better part of a week as he bumped along in the wagon. He was feeling well rested. So, in spite of the fact that it was morning, and in spite of the fact that his arms were tied, he decided to try to get up.

After a long struggle, Gus was able to stand up in the wagon. Just as he stood up, the fearsome beast grunted and charged in to attack. Sir Gus spun around as best he could to see what had made the sound. The bright morning sun shone on his shiny helmet. The sunlight bounced off his helmet and shone on the fearsome beast.

The flash of sunlight shone in the eyes of the fearsome beast and blinded it. The beast screamed and ran away. But it could not see. It ran into the Dark Dismal Swamp and sank in the deep mud.

The bandits, having woken with a start, fled as well. They scrambled into the wagon and drove away as quickly as they could. As they drove off, Gus fell out of the wagon. He landed on the ground with a thud.

Sir Gus the Utterly Fearless lay on the ground for two days, unable to get up. At last a hunter spotted him and untied him.

Sir Gus thanked the hunter. Then he made his way back to the king's palace on foot.

When he arrived, the king was just sitting down for his dinner. Sir Gus knelt and spoke to him.

"Your majesty," he said, "I am happy to report that the fearsome beast lies at the bottom of the Dark Dismal Swamp."

"Well done, Sir Gus!" said the king. "Well done!"

The king called all his knights to a meeting.

"Sir Gus has killed the fearsome beast and tossed its carcass into the Dark Dismal Swamp," the king announced. "Thanks to his brave actions, the kingdom is safe. You may all go home."

The King's Birthday

Six months passed until King Alfred saw his knights. This time he did not need their help, but he asked them to come to his birthday party. The king had asked 500 people to join him. He had made plans for a large feast, as well as jousting, magic, and dancing. Everyone was very excited.

The palace was filled with five thousand candles. Gold cloth was draped on the walls. King Alfred had planned a treat for everyone. Just as the jousting was about to begin, a thousand white doves were to be released into the sky above the palace.

King Alfred asked King Henry, the king of another kingdom, to attend the birthday party. The twelve knights were coming too. King Henry's knights were going to challenge King Alfred's knights in jousting. The winners would get 100 gold coins each.

85

On the day of the party, the king met with some of his knights.

"This is going to be the best party ever!" said the excited king. "I am eager to see each of you joust. I think King Henry and his knights will be amazed by your skill."

"Winning will be our birthday gift to you, Sire!" said Sir Pete.

"We are the most feared knights of all time!" said Sir Tom. "We will crush them! We will make them cry!"

Sir Gus looked on as his fellow knights boasted of their skill. He did not join them. In fact, he was very nervous. He was hoping that he would not start itching and fall off his horse.

"I know you will win," said the king. "And that will make a fine birthday present. I thank you in advance!"

The knights began to file out.

"Sir Gus!" called the king.

"Your majesty?" said Sir Gus.

"Do you like my birthday cake?" asked the king.

"Yes, Sire."

"Do you see how the royal baker made a tiny king out of icing that looks just like me?"

"Yes, Sire."

"It is a wonderful birthday present! But the best present of all will be seeing you defeat Sir Ivan the Black Knight in the jousting."

"Sir Ivan?" asked Sir Gus nervously.

"Yes," said the king. "He has made quite a fearsome name for himself. But I trust you will beat him."

Sir Gus was too scared to speak.

"Well, then," said the king. "Off you go! And happy birthday to me!"

Betrayed

When all of the nobles and knights were assembled in the arena, King Alfred stood up. He welcomed King Henry, who was seated next to him. Then he gave the command to release the doves.

At once a spectacle of white birds rose up into the clear, cloudless sky. The people gasped. Then they clapped and cheered. Finally everyone sat down to see the knights joust.

Sir Ed rode out. He was dressed like a knight prepared for battle. His horse was draped in red, as King Alfred had requested.

His opponent was a knight called Sir Basil. Sir Basil's horse was draped in gold.

Sir Ed smiled at the cheering crowd. When King Alfred gave the command, the jousting began. The rival knights held their lances. Then they charged at each other. Within seconds Sir Ed had knocked Sir Basil to the ground. The crowd stood up and clapped loudly.

Next to enter the arena was Sir Gus. He rode in on the king's horse.

His opponent was Sir Ivan. Sir Ivan was known to be a very fearsome knight. He was called the Black Knight because both he and his horse dressed mostly in black.

Sir Gus and his horse faced the Black Knight. Sir Gus was hoping that he would not begin to itch. He was hoping he would not faint. When the king gave the command, Sir Gus picked up his lance, closed his eyes, and charged at Sir Ivan.

With one blow from the Black Knight's lance, Sir Gus was knocked clean off his horse. He landed on the ground with a thud. His helmet rolled off to one side. The crowd gasped. They waited for their hero, Sir Gus the Utterly Fearless, to get up. But Sir Gus did not get up. He was knocked out, which is just as well really, because what happened next would have scared him to death.

The Wizard

King Henry had a wizard with him. The wizard's name was Albert.

Shortly after Sir Gus was knocked off his horse, Albert the wizard jumped into the arena. Some people hoped that he was going to help Sir Gus, but it soon became clear that he had other plans.

Albert ran into the center of the arena and began to cast a spell. He lifted his arms and screeched out some magic words. Flames rose up into the air. The crowd gasped.

The wizard cast a sleeping spell. The crowd fell asleep. King Alfred and his knights fell asleep, too. The only people who did not fall asleep were King Henry, his knights, and the wizard himself.

You see, King Henry was only pretending to be a good king. In fact, he was a very wicked king. With the help of his wizard and his knights, he hoped to take over King Alfred's kingdom.

King Henry spoke to the Black Knight. He told him to carry King Alfred to the dungeon below the palace. Then King Henry went to say thank you to his wizard.

"Good job, Albert! Well done!" said King Henry. "How long will this spell of yours last?"

"It will last for 100 years," replied Albert, "unless someone finds out how to undo it, and that is very unlikely."

"You see," the wizard explained in a whisper, "there is only one thing that can break the spell and wake everyone up. The web of a male garden spider must be rubbed into King Alfred's left hand. And, as only you and I know the secret, your majesty, it is not going to happen."

King Henry smiled an evil smile and patted his wizard on the back.

Breaking the Spell

Sir Gus awoke to the sound of doves cooing in his ears. He felt the birds rubbing against his chin. Luckily for him, he was asleep when Albert the Wizard cast his spell. Because he was asleep, Sir Gus was not affected by the spell. The doves that were released when the jousting began had come back to the arena and woken him up.

Sir Gus rubbed his eyes. He lifted himself up off the ground. Then he dusted himself off and looked around. He could not quite believe what he saw. The hundreds of people who were clapping and cheering were now fast asleep—all of them!

Just then Sir Gus saw the Black Knight ride past. The Black Knight was carrying a sleeping King Alfred away on his horse.

Sir Gus followed the Black Knight. He saw him carry the king down the steps that led to the palace dungeon.

Sir Gus was confused.

"Goodness, what is happening?" he said to himself.

Sir Gus crept down into the dungeon to look for the king. It was very cold and dark in the dungeon. Sir Gus did not like it one bit. He grabbed a torch to help him see in the dark.

The torch made things even scarier, for it let Sir Gus see all of the scary things in the dungeon. He saw water dripping down from the damp walls. He saw puddles. He saw mice and rats running back and forth. Sir Gus shivered. He did not like mice. Nor was he fond of rats.

The dungeon was filled with cobwebs and scary spiders. The sight of the spiders made Sir Gus tremble and shake.

Sir Gus made his way past lots of cobwebs. In the end he found King Alfred asleep in a tiny cell.

Sir Gus went into the cell. A bat swooped from one dark corner to another. Sir Gus was afraid of bats. He jumped with fright and ran over to the king. The terrified knight reached for the king's left hand. As Sir Gus grabbed it, several strands from the web of a male garden spider were rubbed into the king's left hand. Instantly the king awoke.

Looking for the Enemy

"My good knight, what is happening?" asked an astonished King Alfred, as he got up.

"Your majesty," said Sir Gus, "pardon me, but I am not quite sure. It seems that King Henry and his knights did not come as friends, for I saw the Black Knight place you in this dungeon."

Sir Gus tried to explain as best he could what had happened. However, he could not explain why he had woken up in the jousting arena to find everyone else asleep.

"How are you feeling?" asked the king, recalling that Sir Gus had fallen from his horse in the joust.

"Well, I am still standing," replied Sir Gus.

"We had better get out of here and find out what is happening," said the king.

"Yes," said Sir Gus. "By all means. We must find out what is happening." But, deep down, Sir Gus was not sure he really cared to find out what was happening.

Slowly Sir Gus and the king crept out of the dark dungeon. They set off to find King Alfred's knights.

At the same time the king woke up, so did everyone in the palace and the arena. Slowly people began to realize someone had betrayed King Alfred.

It wasn't long before King Alfred and Sir Gus found the other knights in the palace.

"Your majesty, I rejoice to find you well," said Sir Tom as he knelt and kissed the king's ring. "We feared King Henry had taken you from us. It seems he was planning to take over your kingdom."

"Yes, I am alive, all thanks to Sir Gus," explained the king. "He found me in the palace dungeon. I am still not sure why he found me asleep in my own dungeon."

"That is easy to explain," said Sir Tom. "King Henry's wizard cast a spell that made everyone sleep. It would seem that somehow the spell did not harm Sir Gus, and he was able to wake you up."

"In fact, everyone has woken up," said Sir Ed.

"What about King Henry and his knights?" asked King Alfred. "Where are they?"

"Do not fear, your majesty," said Sir Ed. "We will find King Henry and his knights, and we will see that they are punished for what they have done."

King Alfred's knights looked high and low, and in every corner, for King Henry and his knights. But they were nowhere to be found. Somehow they had all managed to escape.

But at least King Alfred was safe.

Revenge

For a while, King Alfred was very sad. King Henry, his friend, had betrayed him. How could he?

Then King Alfred got mad. *King Henry, his friend, had betrayed him! How dare he?*

When you are a king, you must show your enemies how brave and strong you are. Kings don't do this themselves, as that would be dangerous. They send an army to do it for them. And that is just what King Alfred decided to do.

Late in the afternoon, one month after Albert the Wizard had cast his evil spell, King Alfred held a meeting with his knights. This time all twelve of them arrived on time.

"Sit down," said the king. "I have something important to tell you."

"We are here to serve you," said Sir Tom as, one by one, the knights sat down at a long table.

"I know I have told you how much your bravery means to me," said the king. "I think you are the most excellent knights my kingdom has ever seen, or indeed may ever see."

"Thank you, your majesty," said Sir Ed.

"We rejoice to serve you," said Sir Tom.

"I have decided," explained the king, "that our kingdom must fight King Henry's kingdom. We must strike back! We must punish him for his treason and evil deeds!"

"If I may say so," said Sir Ed, "that is an excellent idea!"

"Indeed!" said Sir Tom. "We should show him who's boss around here!"

"Just what I was thinking," replied the king, "and that is why I have decided to send an army to fight against King Henry's army. I won't lead the army myself, you know."

"No, indeed not," agreed Sir Tom. "That would be silly."

"Yes, very silly indeed," said the king with a smile. "No, our most respected knight, the leader among leaders, the fighter among fighters, will lead the army. My other brave knights will assist him."

Eleven of the twelve knights looked at each other eagerly. Each of them was hoping that the king was going to pick him to lead the army. As the king was about to say which knight he had picked, Sir Gus fell off his chair.

The reason for his fall is easy to explain. That afternoon, after eating a large lunch, Sir Gus went to sit in the king's rose garden. It was there that he was stung by a bee. The bee had stung him on the bottom, and he was finding it very difficult to sit down. In the end, the pain was too much for him. He fell off his chair and landed in front of the king.

Battle Plans

"Yes, I pick you, Sir Gus! Why, who else would I pick?" said the king. "I have lost count of all the times you have saved me."

You see, the king believed Sir Gus had fallen off his chair in his eagerness to volunteer to lead the army.

"You must get started, Sir Gus," the king went on. "You must prepare your army. The other good knights will assist you with your battle plans. Good luck!"

With those words, the king left the room and went off to walk his dog.

Sir Gus was stunned.

"Me?" he mumbled.

"Yes, you!" shouted all eleven knights together.

Sir Tom reached for a map of King Henry's kingdom.

"You will need this," said Sir Tom. He was feeling a little sad that King Alfred had not chosen him, but what could he do?

"This map shows all of the hills, rivers, and valleys in King Henry's kingdom," Sir Tom explained.

"Thank you," said Sir Gus. He did not understand why he would need a map that showed hills, rivers, and valleys, unless it was to point out the best places to hide. Still, he took the map and pretended to look at it.

"Sir Gus," said Sir Tom, "you are holding the map upside down."

"Am I?" said Sir Gus. Then he added, "Yes, I am. You see, I am trying to get a sense of how things might look from the enemy's position."

"What is your plan?" asked Sir Ed. Like Sir Tom, he was sad that he was not chosen to lead the attack. But there was not much he could do about it. "Do you plan a sudden attack at night with some of the army, or an all-out attack at sunrise with the entire army?"

"Sunrise?" said Sir Gus. "That is in the morning. No, I think the attack at night is a much better plan. If you like, Sir Ed, you could lead the sudden attack, and I could stay with the rest of the army and keep them safe."

"I could not take this moment of glory away from you," said Sir Ed. "It would not be fair."

"Sure, you can," replied Sir Gus. "I mean, you must not feel bad. I have other plans up my sleeve—plans that will soon be revealed."

"Well, if you really don't mind," said Sir Ed, "I would be delighted."

Sir Ed was starting to feel much happier about everything.

"I have just one request," said Sir Ed.

"Yes," said Sir Gus. "What is it?"

"The Black Knight and his men are camped in the Fields of the West," explained Sir Ed. "I would like to attack them there. And I would like to take Sir Tom with me. He can lead our knights in battle, while I lead our foot troops."

"I was just about to say the very same thing," announced Sir Gus.

"Wonderful!" said Sir Ed. "Excellent!"

"Splendid!" said Sir Tom. "Fantastic!"

By this point, Sir Tom and Sir Ed were both feeling a lot happier.

"It seems we have a good plan," said Sir Tom. "We will go and get the horses."

"Good idea," said Sir Gus. "I will stay here and make sure the rest of the army stays safe."

Eleven of the knights went off to prepare for battle. Sir Gus went off to find someone who could stop the awful pain he was feeling in his bottom.

Marching Orders

The next morning, the knight known as Sir Doug arrived at the palace. He found Sir Gus in the king's kitchen cooking eggs and bacon.

"Good morning!" said a cheery Sir Gus.

"Sir Gus," cried Sir Doug, "Sir Tom and Sir Ed need your help!"

"They do?" said Sir Gus, who was beginning to suspect that there would be no time to eat breakfast.

"Yes!" replied Sir Doug. "Their sudden night attack in the Fields of the West did not go well. They were engaged in fierce fighting with the Black Knight. They have battled all night. They sent me to beg you to come with the rest of the army and save them! Sir Gus, the rest of the army is awaiting your command."

"Yes, indeed, my command," replied Sir Gus, knowing that he must go at once. "Go and saddle the horses! We will ride at once!"

A little while later, Sir Gus appeared in front of the king's palace. He was dressed for battle and holding the map Sir Tom had given him.

"My friends," Sir Gus announced, "we will ride south, until we get to the Old Stone Bridge. Then we will use the bridge to cross the Misty River and enter King Henry's kingdom."

Sir Doug and the rest of the men looked puzzled.

"But, Sir Gus," said Sir Doug, "the Old Stone Bridge is north of here, not south."

"Is it?" said Sir Gus. "Then we will ride north."

"Very well," said Sir Doug. "But, if you don't mind my asking, Sir Gus, why should we ride all the way up to the Old Stone Bridge? That will take us ten miles away from the fighting. Sir Ed and Sir Tom need us. Would it not be better to take the quickest way? The battle is just west of here. If we ride west to the river, we can dismount and walk our horses across the river."

"It is too dangerous," Sir Gus said.

What Sir Gus did not tell them was that he did not know how to swim and was frightened to cross the river on foot.

And that was the real reason why Sir Gus and his men rode north.

The Final Battle

Sir Gus and his men rode north. They reached the Old Stone Bridge just as the sun began to set. There they rested.

Meanwhile the Black Knight waited in the Fields of the West. He had taken Sir Tom and Sir Ed prisoner. He was sure King Alfred would send the rest of his army to try to free them. He was sure that King Alfred's army would come charging across the shallow waters of the Misty River and attack him in the Fields of the West.

The Black Knight placed his men along the banks of the river. He kept them on high alert all day. They waited and waited. But King Alfred's army never came.

Late in the afternoon, the Black Knight told his men to stand down.

"It appears that King Alfred has given up!" he told his men. "Let us march back to the palace."

Then he spoke to his prisoners, Sir Tom and Sir Ed. "King Alfred must not care about you," said the Black Knight. "We will take you back to King Henry and let him decide what to do with you."

The Black Knight and his men began their march. They felt the fighting was finished. They took off their helmets. They tossed their shields and weapons into the supply wagons. The men began to smile and relax and pat each other on the back. They were not expecting what happened next.

When the battle was won, the men cried, "King Alfred is the greatest king, and Sir Gus is the bravest knight of all!"

They grabbed Sir Gus and tossed him high in the air, shouting "Hooray for Sir Gus! Hooray for Sir Gus!"

About this Book

This book has been created for use by students learning to read with the Core Knowledge Language Arts. Readability levels are suitable for early readers. The book has also been carefully leveled in terms of its "code load," or the number of spellings used in the stories.

The English writing system is complex. It uses more than 200 spellings to stand for 40-odd sounds. Many sounds can be spelled several different ways, and many spellings can be pronounced several different ways. This book has been designed to make early reading experiences easier and more productive by using a subset of the available spellings. It uses *only* spellings that students have been taught to sound out as part of their phonics lessons, plus a handful of tricky words, which have also been deliberately introduced in the lessons. This means that the stories will be 100% decodable if they are assigned at the proper time.

As the students move through the program, they learn new spellings and the "code load" in the decodable readers increases gradually. The code load graphics on this page indicate the number of spellings students are expected to know in order to read the first story of the book and the number of spellings students are expected to know in order to read the final stories in the book. The columns on the inside back cover list the specific spellings and tricky words students are expected to recognize at the beginning of this reader. The bullets at the bottom of the inside back cover identify spellings, tricky words, and other topics that are introduced gradually in the unit this reader is designed to accompany.

Visit us on the web at www.coreknowledge.org

Core Knowledge Language Arts

Series Editor-in-Chief
E. D. Hirsch, Jr.

President
Linda Bevilacqua

Editorial Staff
Carolyn Gosse, Senior Editor - Preschool
Khara Turnbull, Materials Development Manager
Michelle L. Warner, Senior Editor - Listening & Learning

Mick Anderson
Robin Blackshire
Maggie Buchanan
Paula Coyner
Sue Fulton
Sara Hunt
Erin Kist
Robin Luecke
Rosie McCormick
Cynthia Peng
Liz Pettit
Ellen Sadler
Deborah Samley
Diane Auger Smith
Sarah Zelinke

Design and Graphics Staff
Scott Ritchie, Creative Director

Kim Berrall
Michael Donegan
Liza Greene
Matt Leech
Bridget Moriarty
Lauren Pack

Consulting Project Management Services
ScribeConcepts.com

Additional Consulting Services
Ang Blanchette
Dorrit Green
Carolyn Pinkerton

Acknowledgments

These materials are the result of the work, advice, and encouragement of numerous individuals over many years. Some of those singled out here already know the depth of our gratitude; others may be surprised to find themselves thanked publicly for help they gave quietly and generously for the sake of the enterprise alone. To helpers named and unnamed we are deeply grateful.

Contributors to Earlier Versions of these Materials
Susan B. Albaugh, Kazuko Ashizawa, Nancy Braier, Kathryn M. Cummings, Michelle De Groot, Diana Espinal, Mary E. Forbes, Michael L. Ford, Ted Hirsch, Danielle Knecht, James K. Lee, Diane Henry Leipzig, Martha G. Mack, Liana Mahoney, Isabel McLean, Steve Morrison, Juliane K. Munson, Elizabeth B. Rasmussen, Laura Tortorelli, Rachael L. Shaw, Sivan B. Sherman, Miriam E. Vidaver, Catherine S. Whittington, Jeannette A. Williams

We would like to extend special recognition to Program Directors Matthew Davis and Souzanne Wright who were instrumental to the early development of this program.

Schools
We are truly grateful to the teachers, students, and administrators of the following schools for their willingness to field test these materials and for their invaluable advice: Capitol View Elementary, Challenge Foundation Academy (IN), Community Academy Public Charter School, Lake Lure Classical Academy, Lepanto Elementary School, New Holland Core Knowledge Academy, Paramount School of Excellence, Pioneer Challenge Foundation Academy, New York City PS 26R (The Carteret School), PS 30X (Wilton School), PS 50X (Clara Barton School), PS 96Q, PS 102X (Joseph O. Loretan), PS 104Q (The Bays Water), PS 214K (Michael Friedsam), PS 223Q (Lyndon B. Johnson School), PS 308K (Clara Cardwell), PS 333Q (Goldie Maple Academy), Sequoyah Elementary School, South Shore Charter Public School, Spartanburg Charter School, Steed Elementary School, Thomas Jefferson Classical Academy, Three Oaks Elementary, West Manor Elementary.

And a special thanks to the CKLA Pilot Coordinators Anita Henderson, Yasmin Lugo-Hernandez, and Susan Smith, whose suggestions and day-to-day support to teachers using these materials in their classrooms was critical.

CREDITS

WRITERS
Rosie McCormick

ILLUSTRATORS AND IMAGE SOURCES
All illustrations by Jacob Wyatt